For my gastroenterologist, Dr. Bortuzzo.
—A. R.

For Loup Emile, Rafe, and Felix.
—L. P.

Library of Congress Cataloging-in-Publication Data available.

ISBN 978-1-4521-8386-2

Manufactured in China.

MIX
Paper from
responsible sources
FSC
www.fsc.org
FSC™ C104723

Design by Jay Marvel.
Typeset in Brandon Grotesque, Slappy, and Archer.
The illustrations in this book were rendered digitally.

10 9 8 7 6 5 4 3 2 1

Chronicle Books LLC
680 Second Street
San Francisco, California 94107

Chronicle Books—we see things differently.
Become part of our community at www.chroniclekids.com.

DIGESTION!
THE MUSICAL

Written by **Adam Rex**

Illustrated by **Laura Park**

chronicle books
san francisco

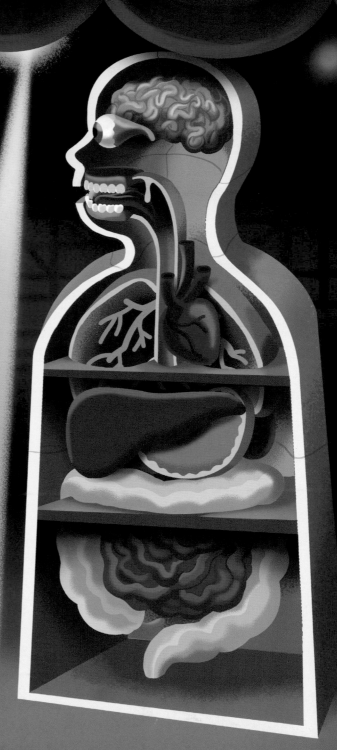

Your bones hold up
your muscles,
and your muscles
make you go.

And your heart will
have to hustle
just to get your blood to
flow around your

BODY!

BODY!

BODY!

BODY!

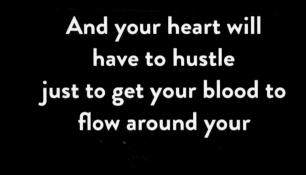

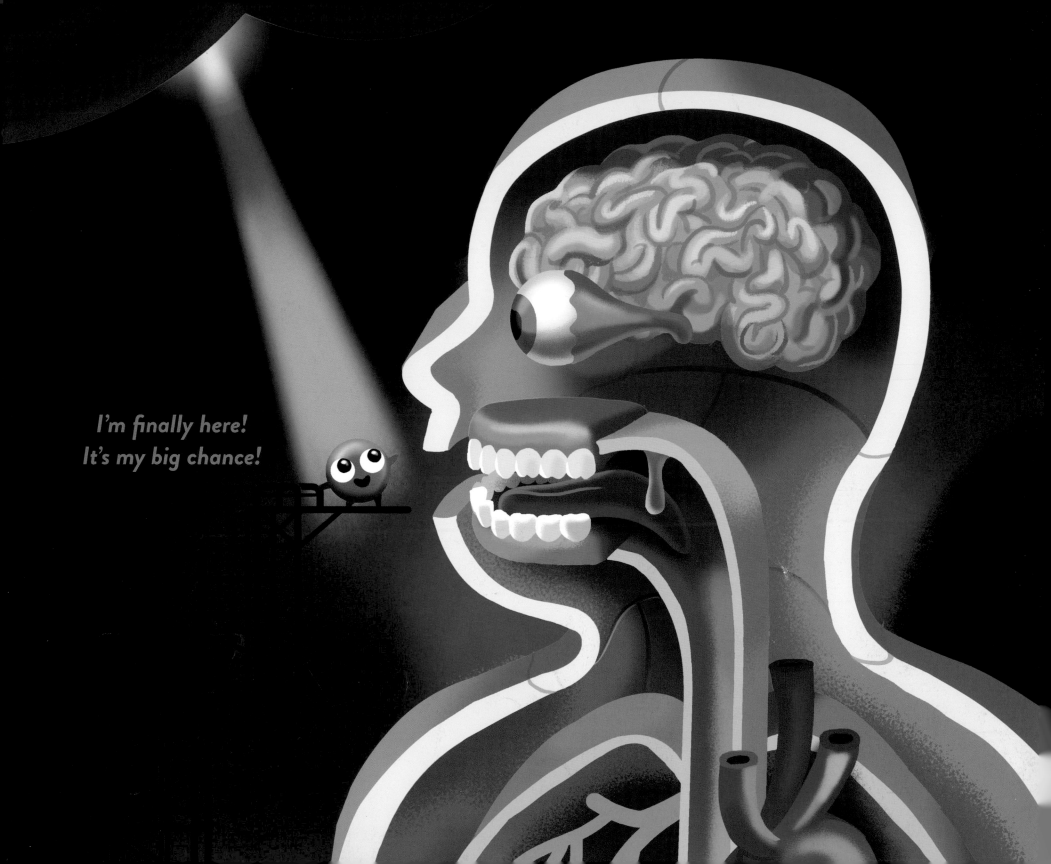

Inside this body I am going to be something— something important!

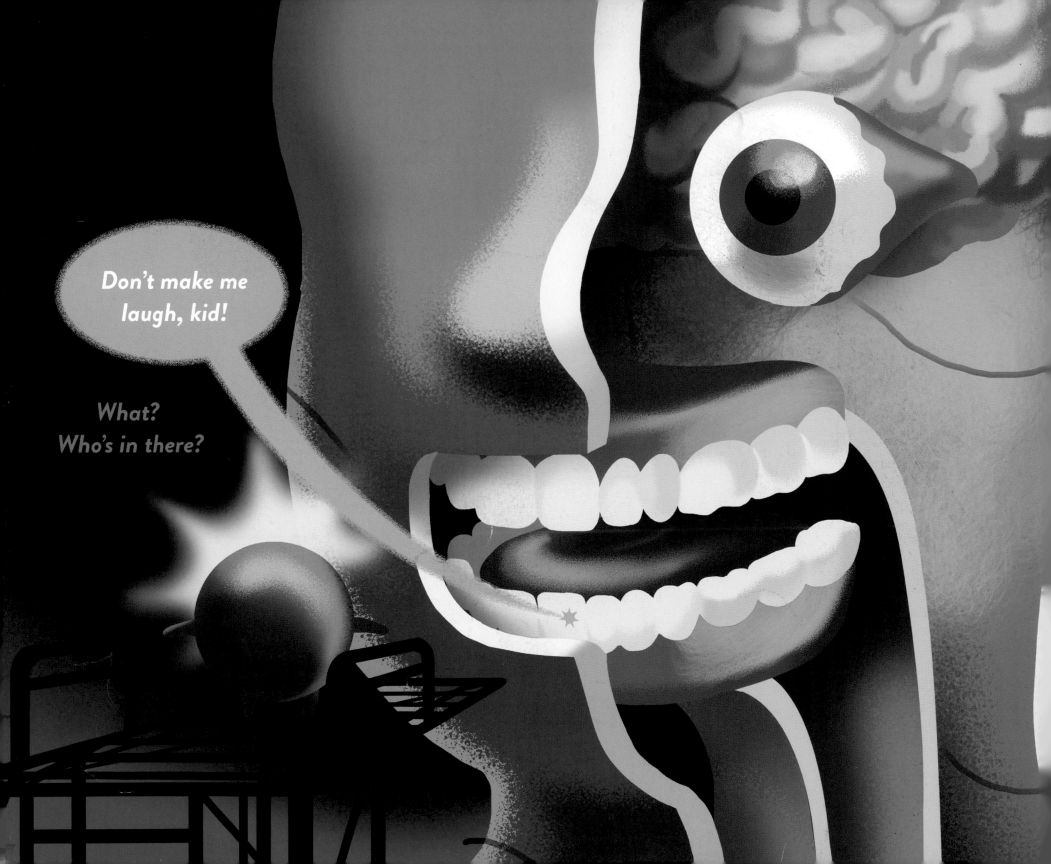

You're junk! Empty calories!

You'll never make anything of yourself here!

Your blood goes to a boo-boo, and a boo-boo gives you pain. So your nerves will send the message of the pain up to your brain inside your

BODY! BODY!
BODY!
BODY!

Thank you!
I won't let you down!

I *think she has good taste.*

Ugh . . . fine.
You can come in,
but don't expect
us teeth to help you—
you're on your
own, kid.

The brain is sent a signal that the
tummy wants a treat,

so it tells the mouth to
open up and welcome
something sweet inside the

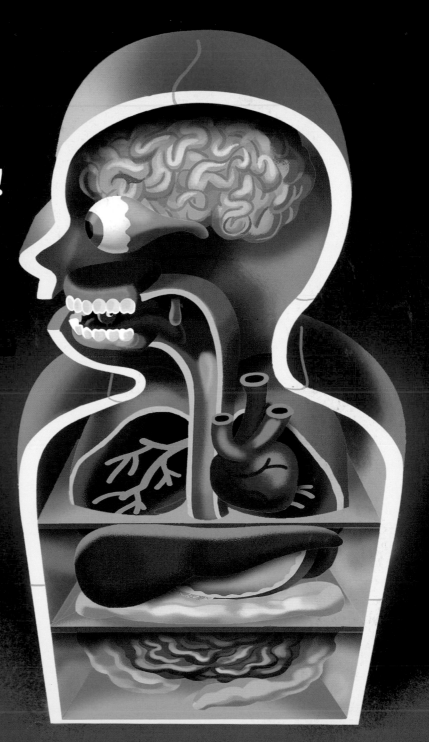

The Chronicle Books Theatre proudly presents

DIGESTION!
THE MUSICAL

A REVUE TO FOLLOW
WHAT WE CHEW AND SWALLOW

starring
YOUR BODY

featuring
**LI'L CANDY
GUM**

and the
**BABY CARROT
SINGERS**

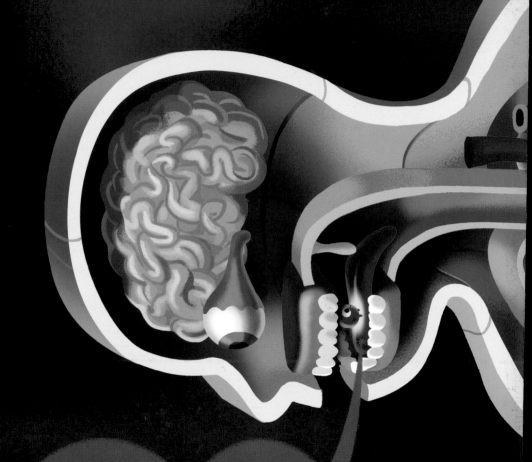

My
um nasha
dada fawa.
Mut I modda
dooey shoo?

Mannan affa
dada swawa?
I sha wadda
wamma doo?

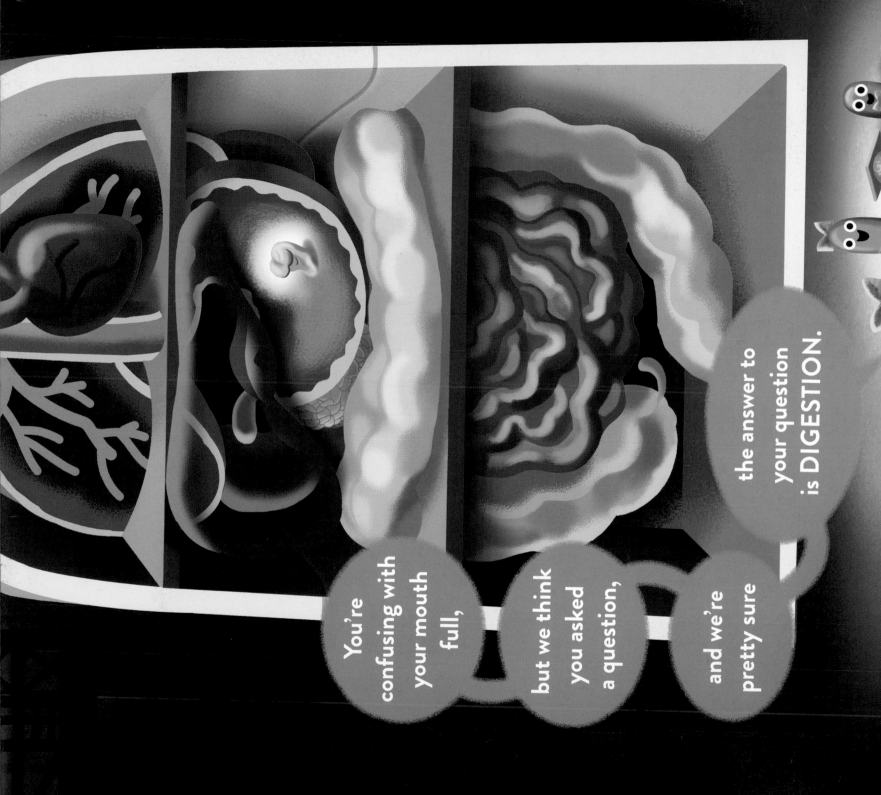

If there's something in your mouth that you can eat, then that's digestion.

It starts when food is chewed—

then swallowing is following—

it mixes in the stomach for an hour, maybe two.

BRAIN

EYE

TONGUE

TEETH

ESOPHAGUS

HEART

LUNGS

STOMACH

KIDNEYS

GALL-BLADDER

LIVER

PANCREAS

LARGE INTESTINE

SMALL INTESTINE

RECTUM

APPENDIX

Then it finishes digestin' in the small and large intestines,

and the garbage that's left over leaves the body when you poo.

You can giggle at that last part, but we mean it, 'cause it's true.

(Okay.)

DIGESTION!
(What? What?)

DIGESTION!
(Hooray!)

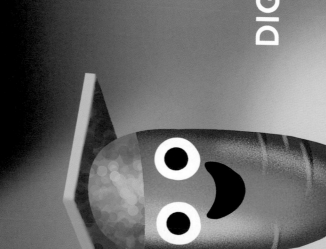

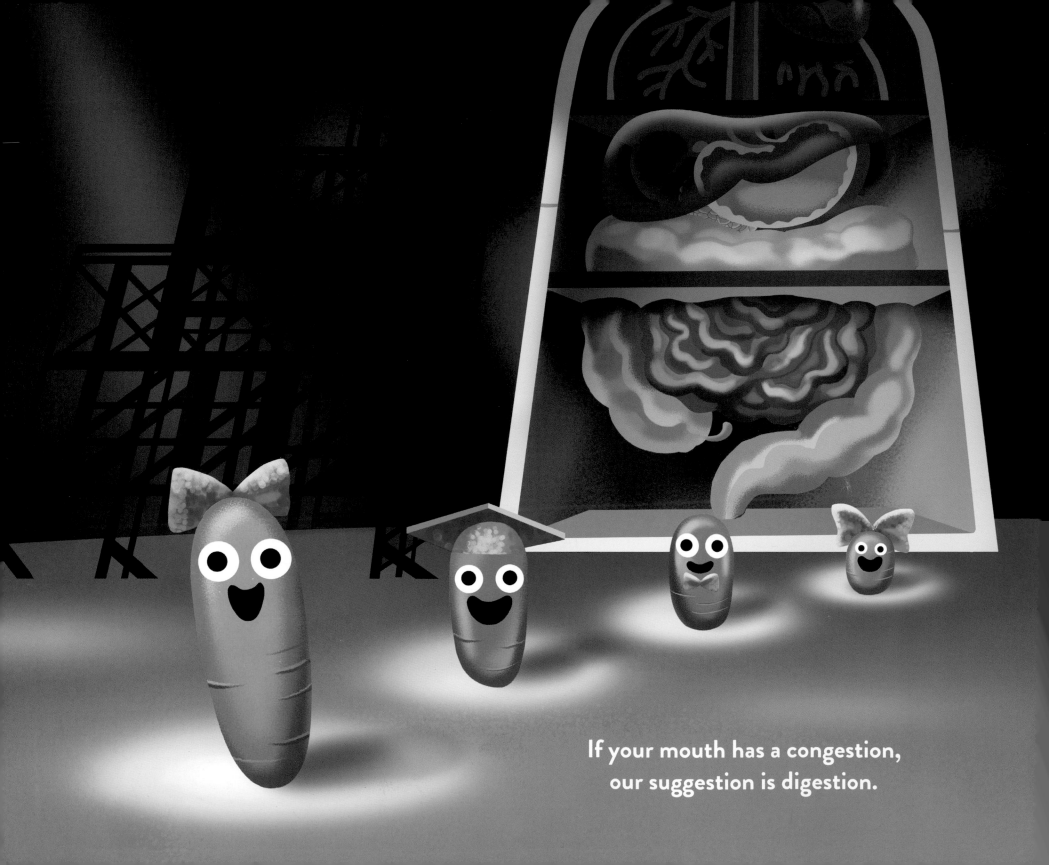

If your mouth has a congestion,
our suggestion is digestion.

We've done our introductions,
and the title song is sung,
so let's check on Li'l Candy,
sitting sweetly on the tongue.

That's her cue, but she's debuting
in a mouth that isn't doing
what it really should be doing—

which is chewing

which is chewing.

ACT 2

Tonight's the night—
finally someone with
an appetite!

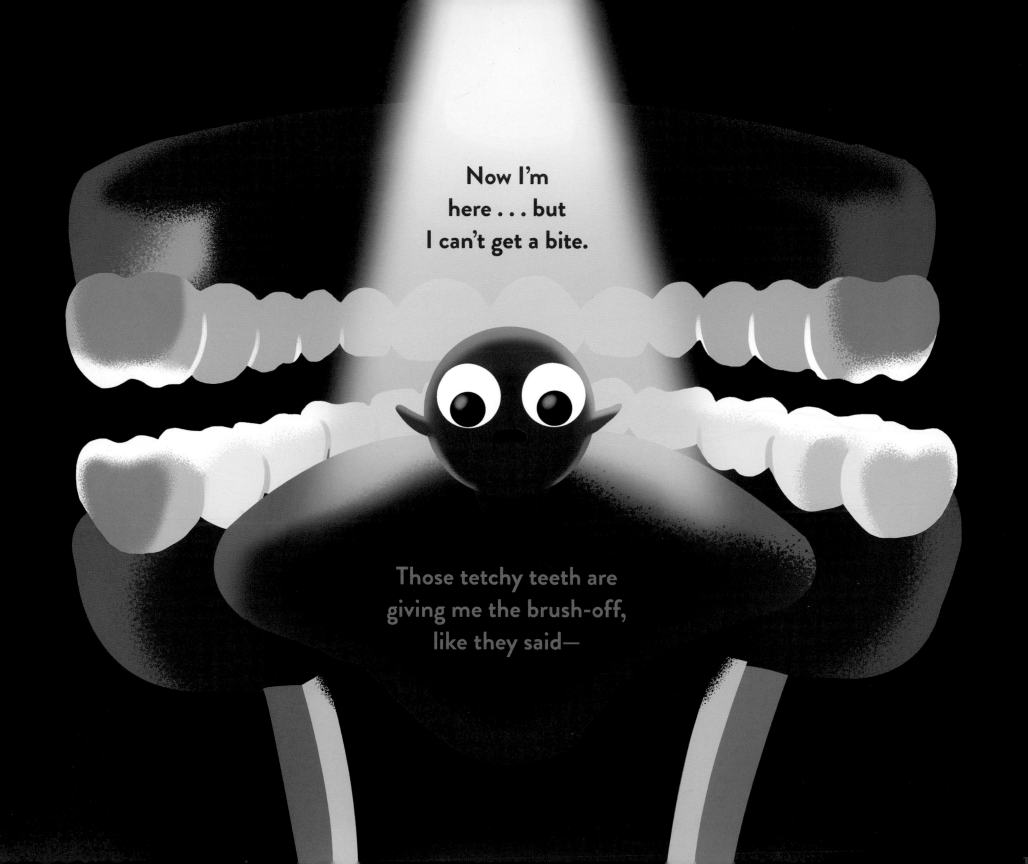

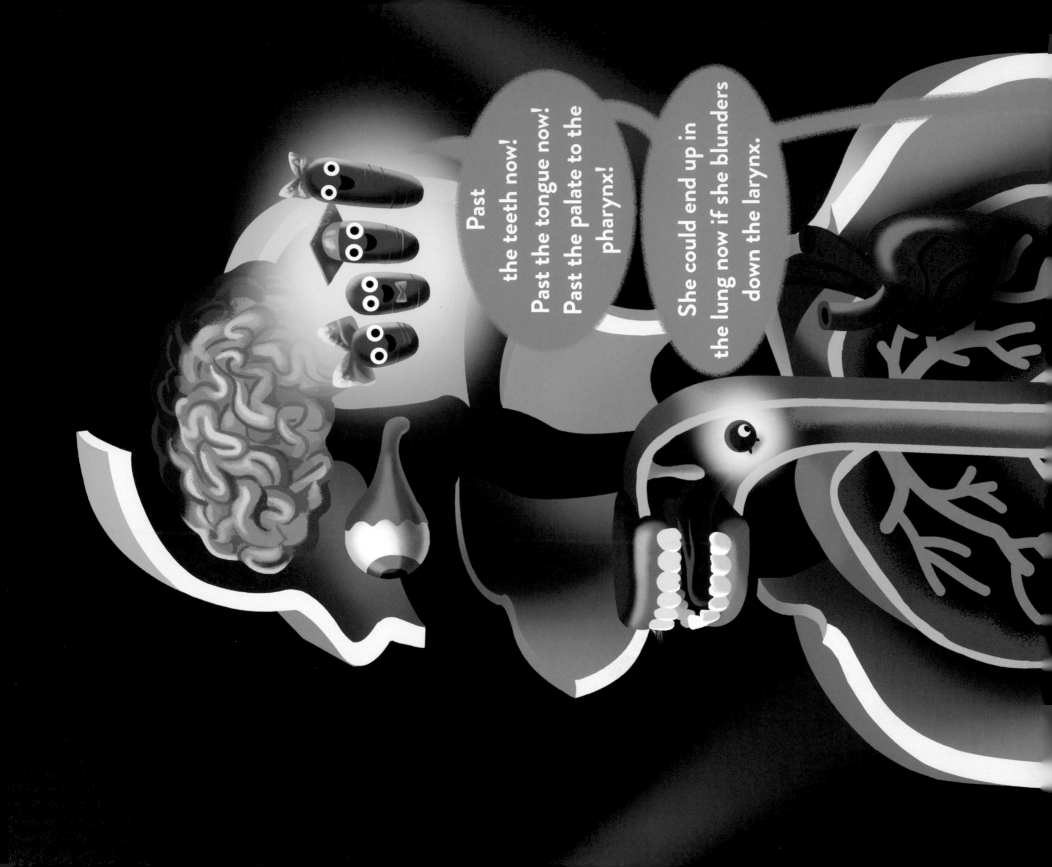

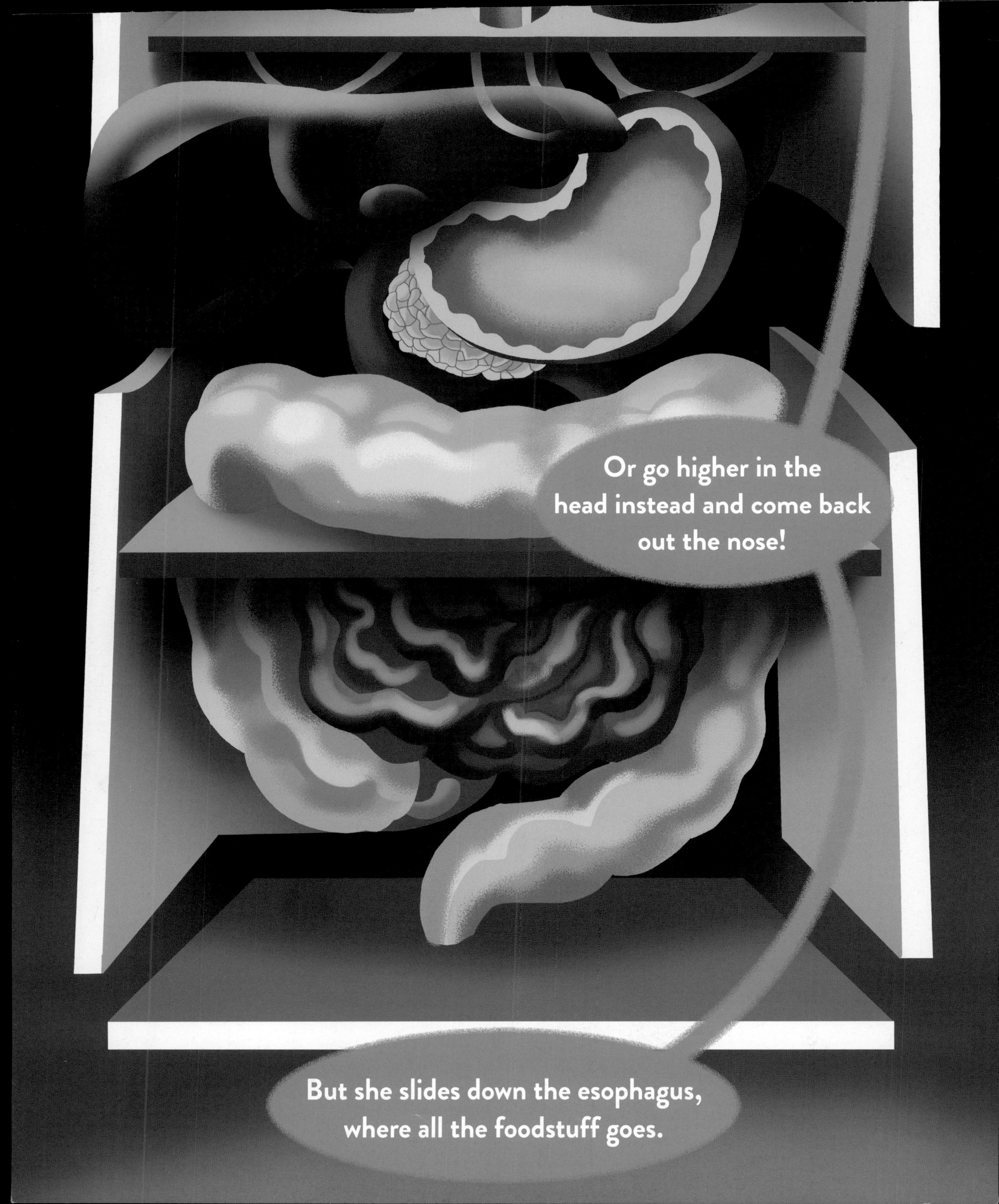
Or go higher in the head instead and come back out the nose!
But she slides down the esophagus, where all the foodstuff goes.

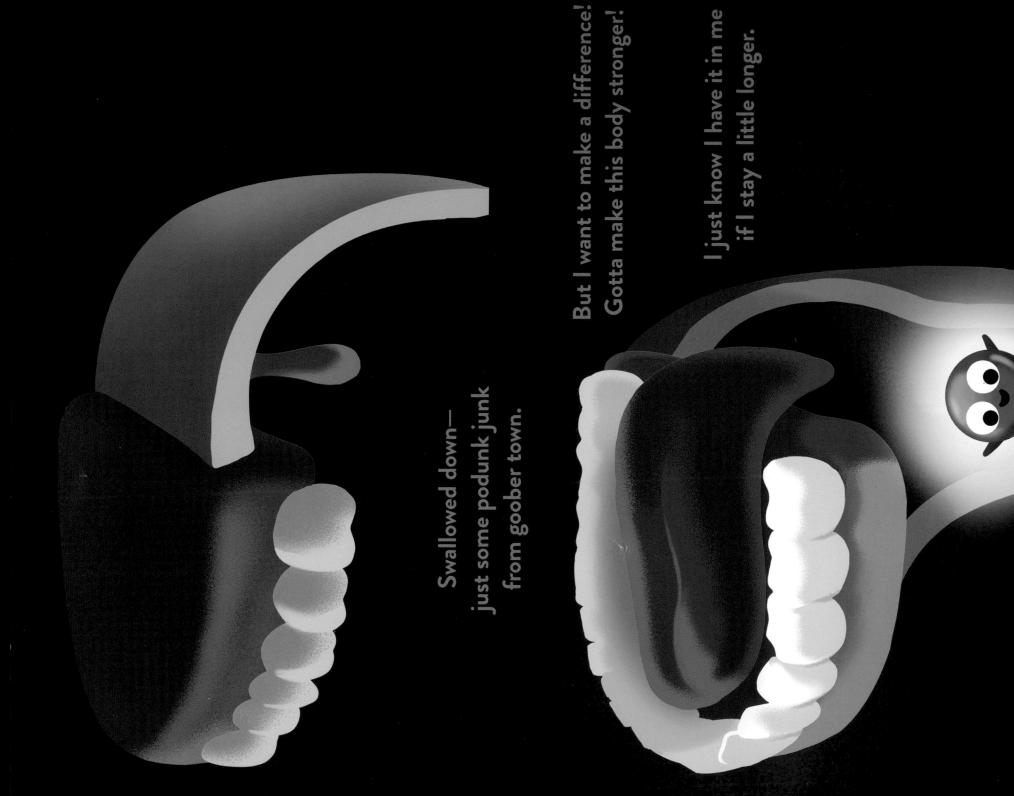

Swallowed down—
just some podunk junk
from goober town.

But I want to make a difference!
Gotta make this body stronger!

I just know I have it in me
if I stay a little longer.

That's the spirit! Good for Candy, with her optimistic thinking.

But her hopeful heart is soaring while the rest of her is sinking.

The esophagus has muscles, and they ripple like a jelly; it makes waves called peristalsis that she rides down to the belly.

Surfin' the esophagus!

Surfin' the esophagus!

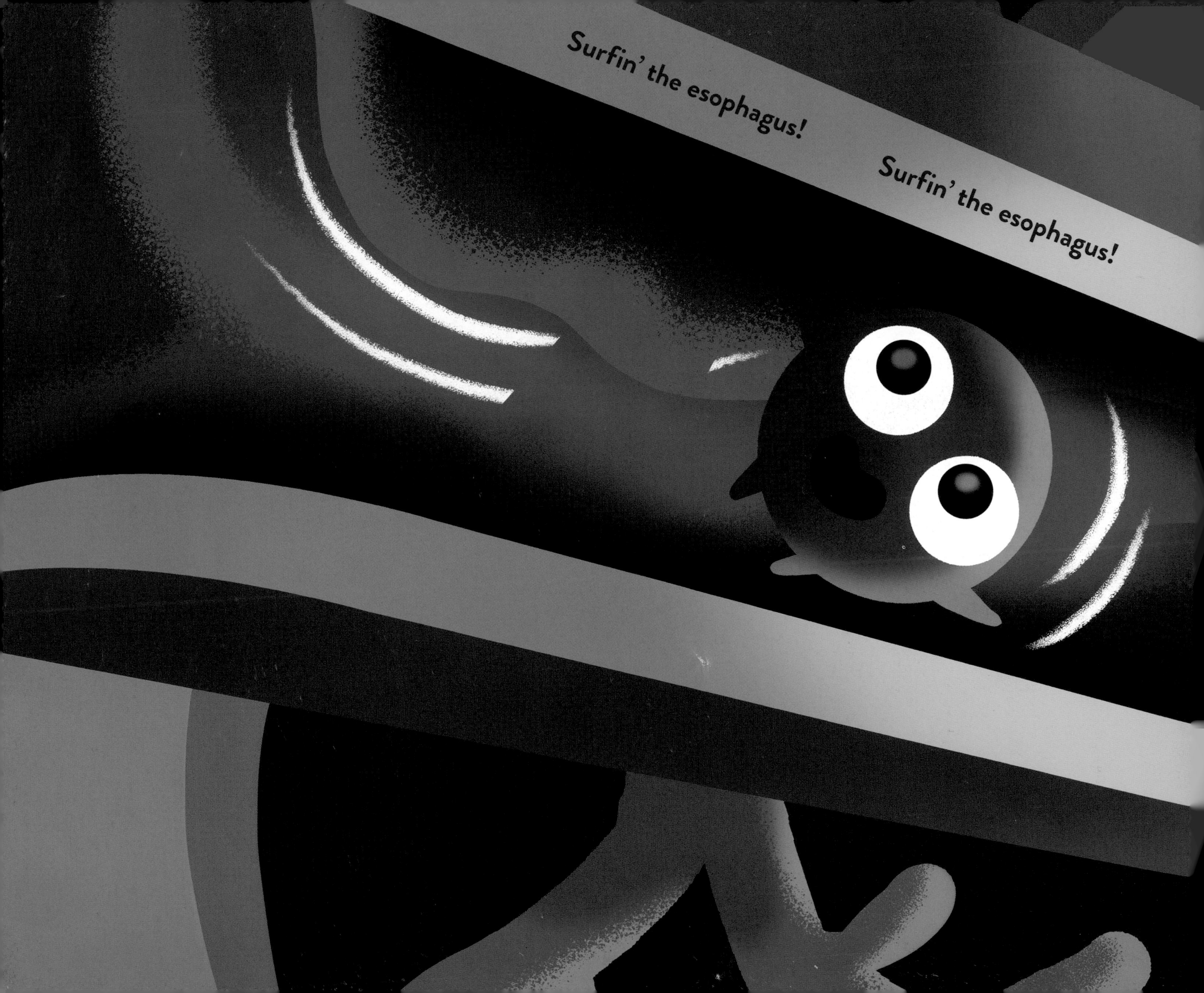

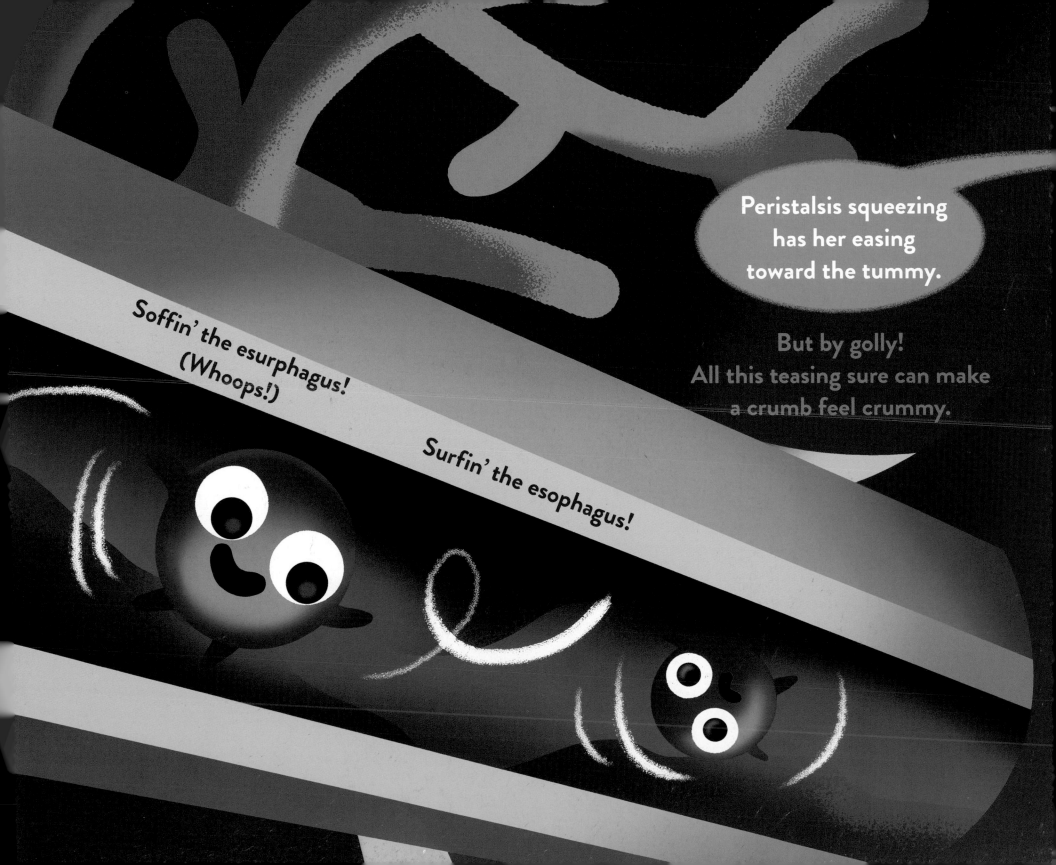

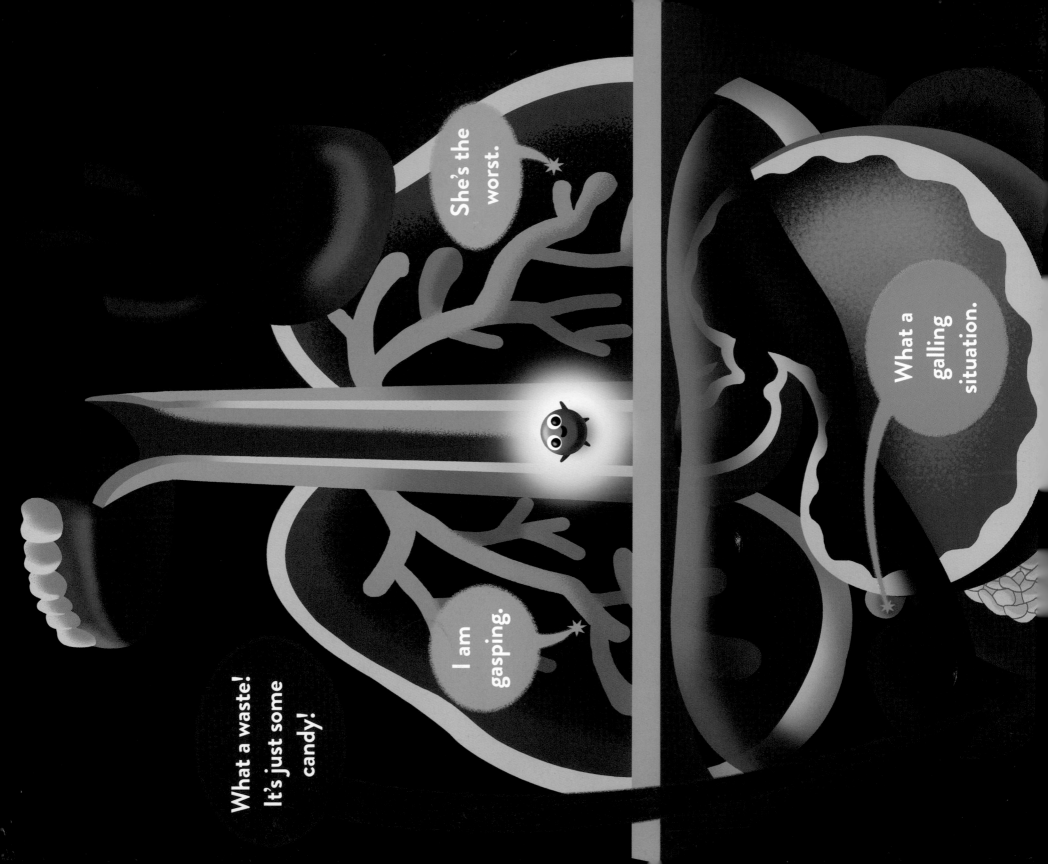

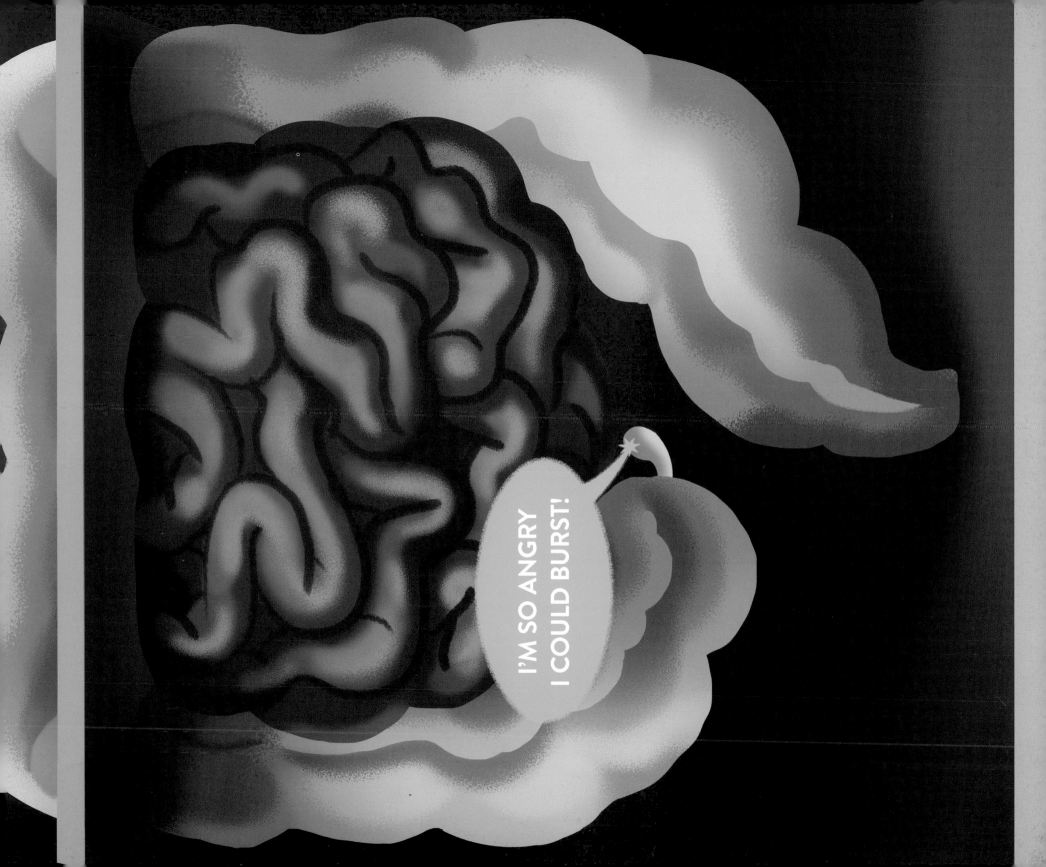

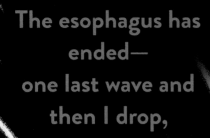

The esophagus has ended—
one last wave and
then I drop,

and I splash
into the mash
inside the
stomach,
where I stop.

What . . . what
is this stuff?

Digestive juices, kid!
They're gonna turn you
into goop!

Whoa!

What's
happening?

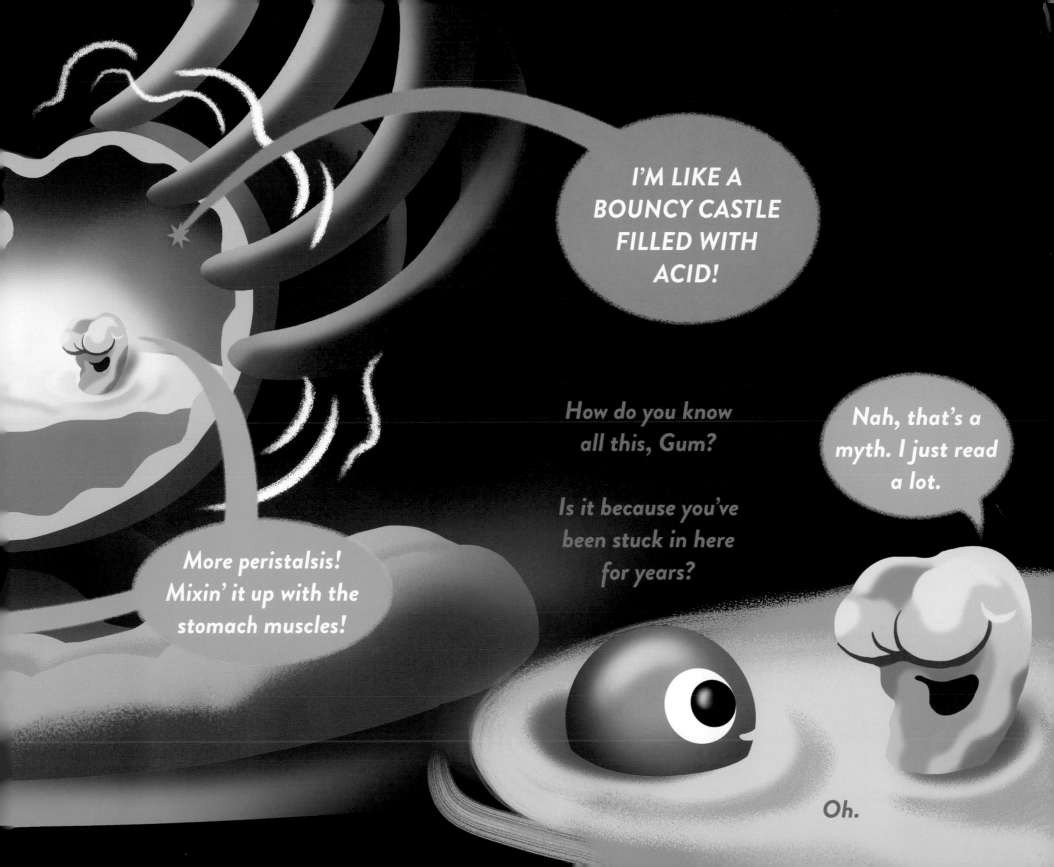

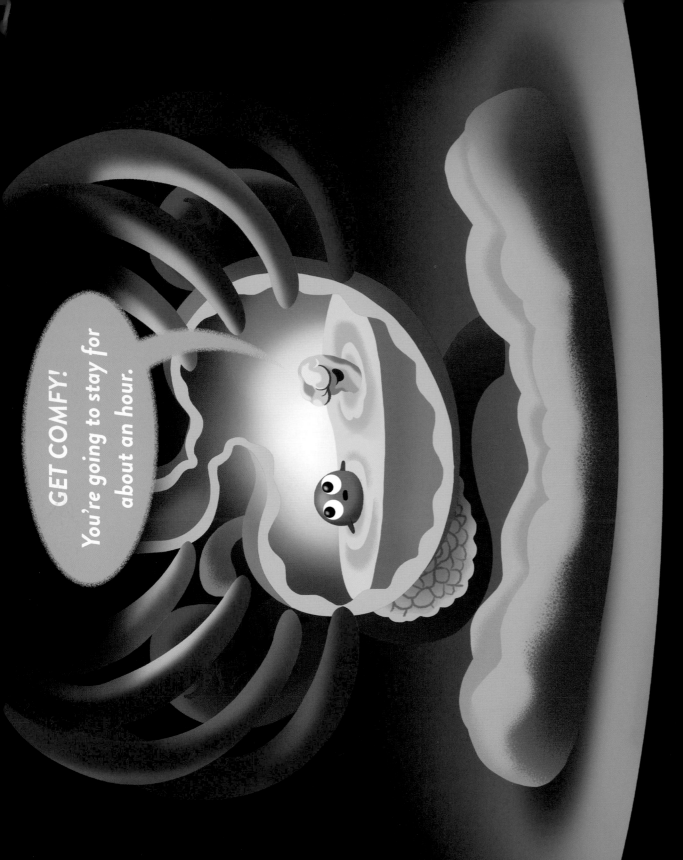
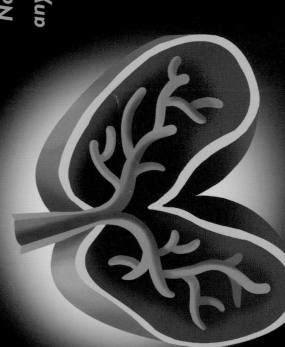

You're our number one problem, Candy!

So keep moving, you good-for-nothing!

You bilious bonbon!

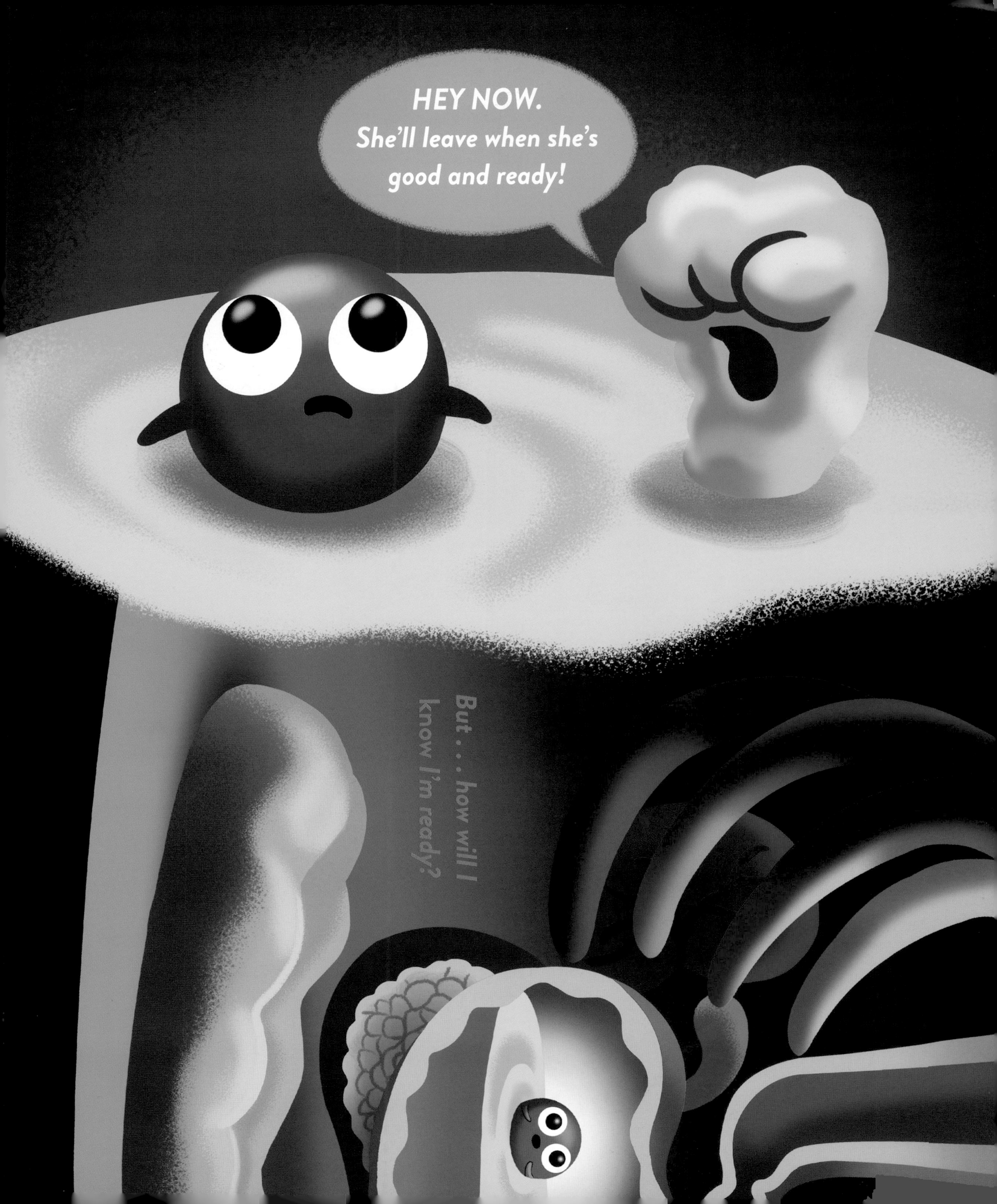
HEY NOW.
She'll leave when she's good and ready!
But . . . how will I know I'm ready?

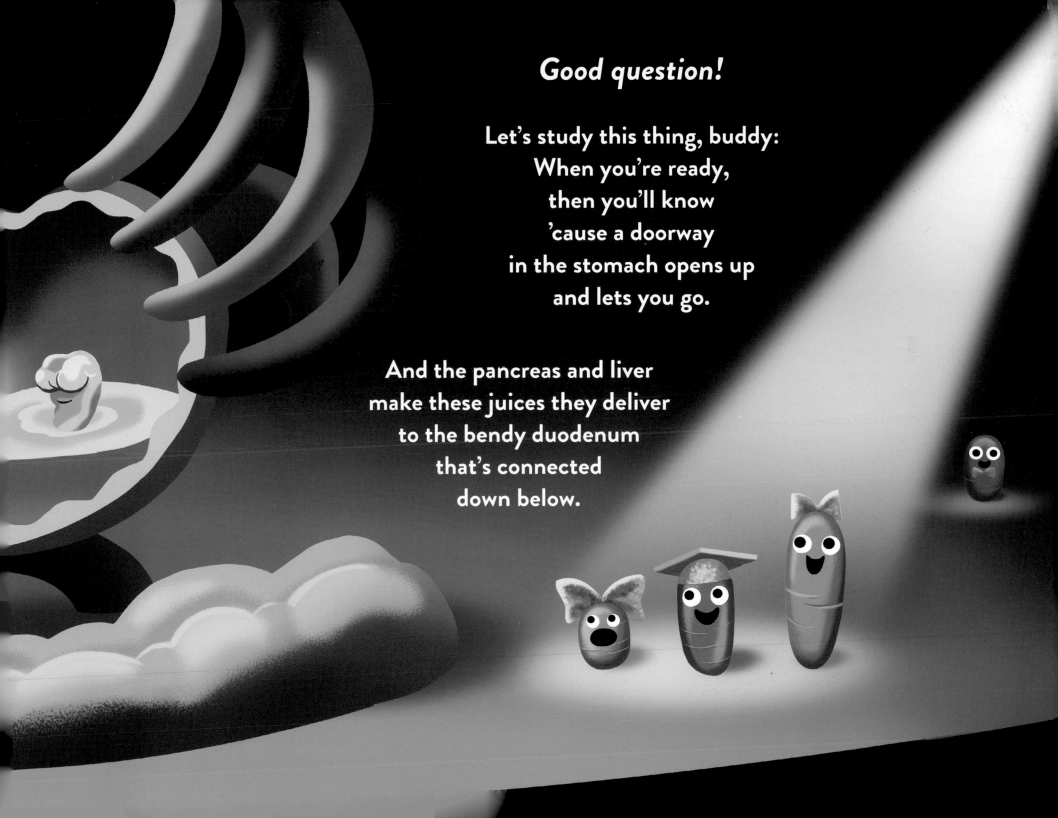

Good question!

Let's study this thing, buddy:
When you're ready,
then you'll know
'cause a doorway
in the stomach opens up
and lets you go.

And the pancreas and liver
make these juices they deliver
to the bendy duodenum
that's connected
down below.

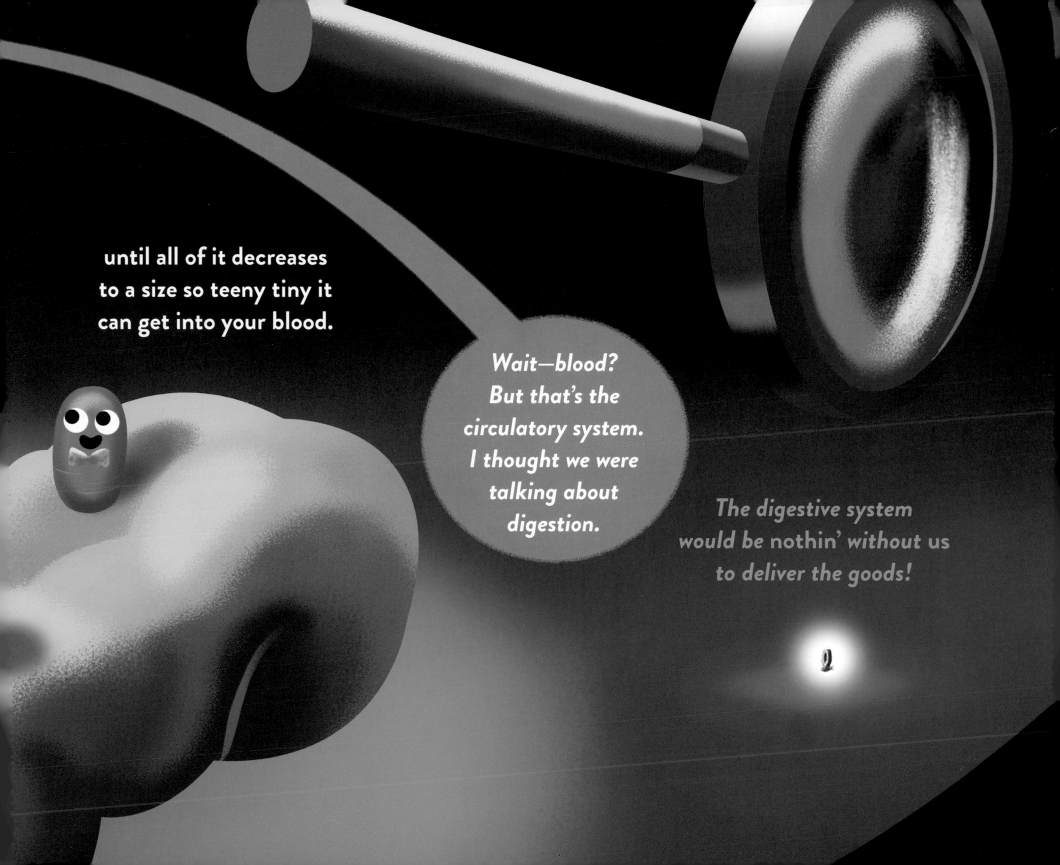

Who said that?

Aw, it's just me—
Little Red Blood Cell! I deliver oxygen from
the lungs so the body can
breathe, which reminds me—I gotta go!

Tell 'em what you do, everyone!

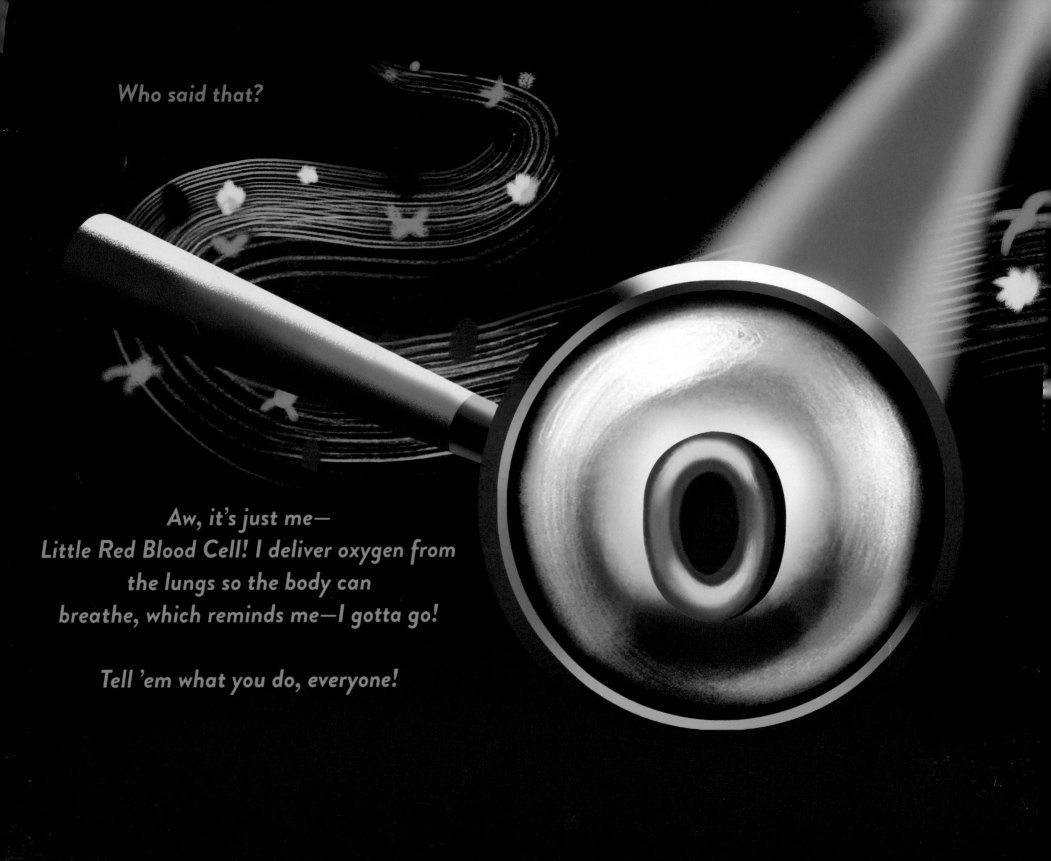

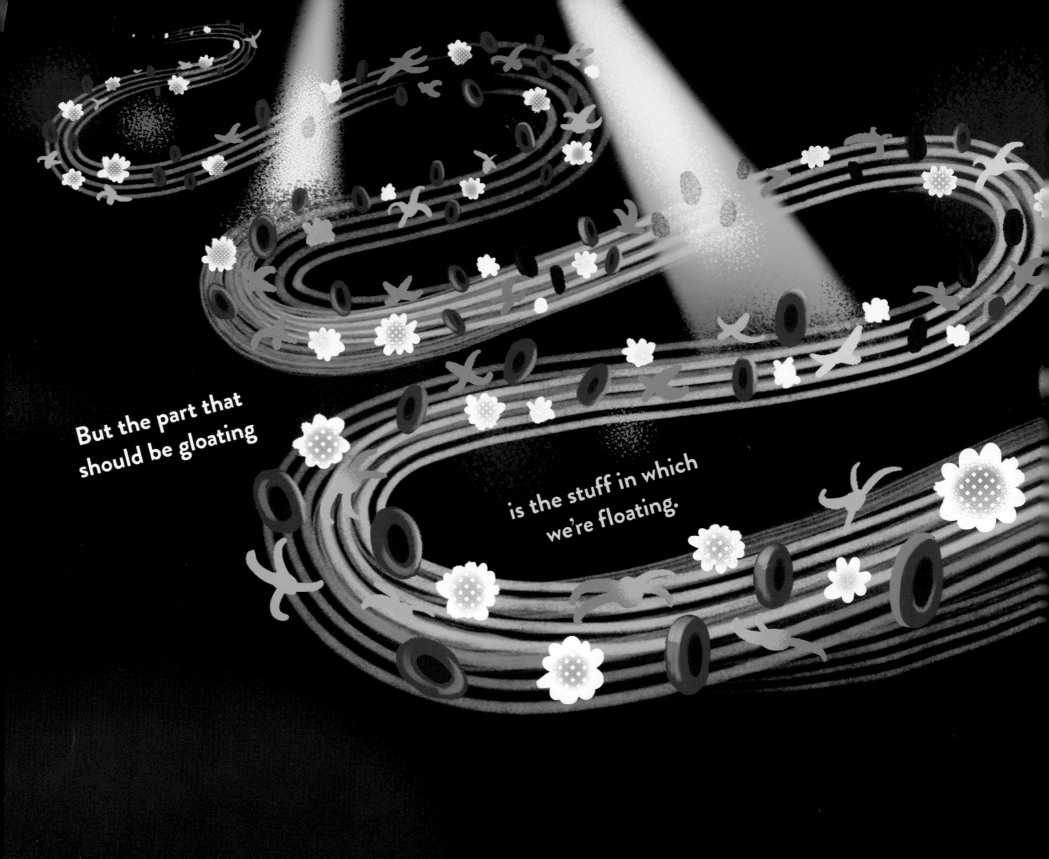

But the part that
should be gloating

is the stuff in which
we're floating.

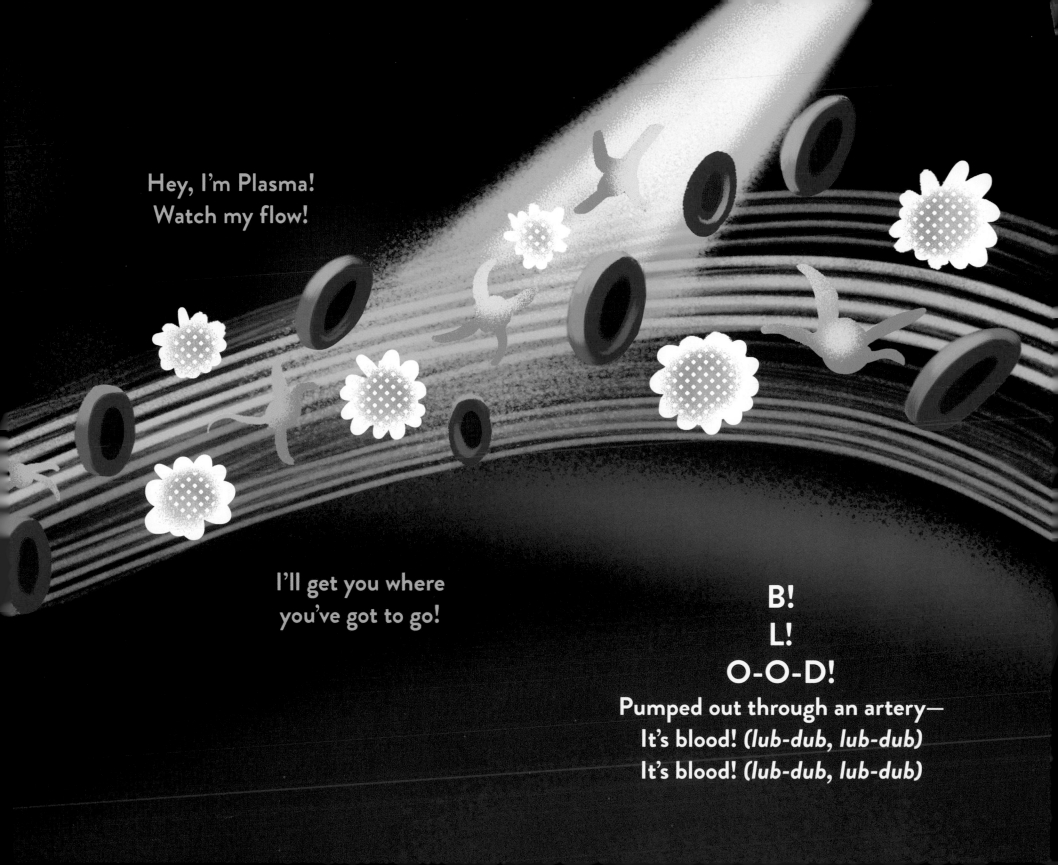

I'm back!
I travel all around this big body, day in, day out. It's the heart that makes it happen.

Okay, back in a minute!

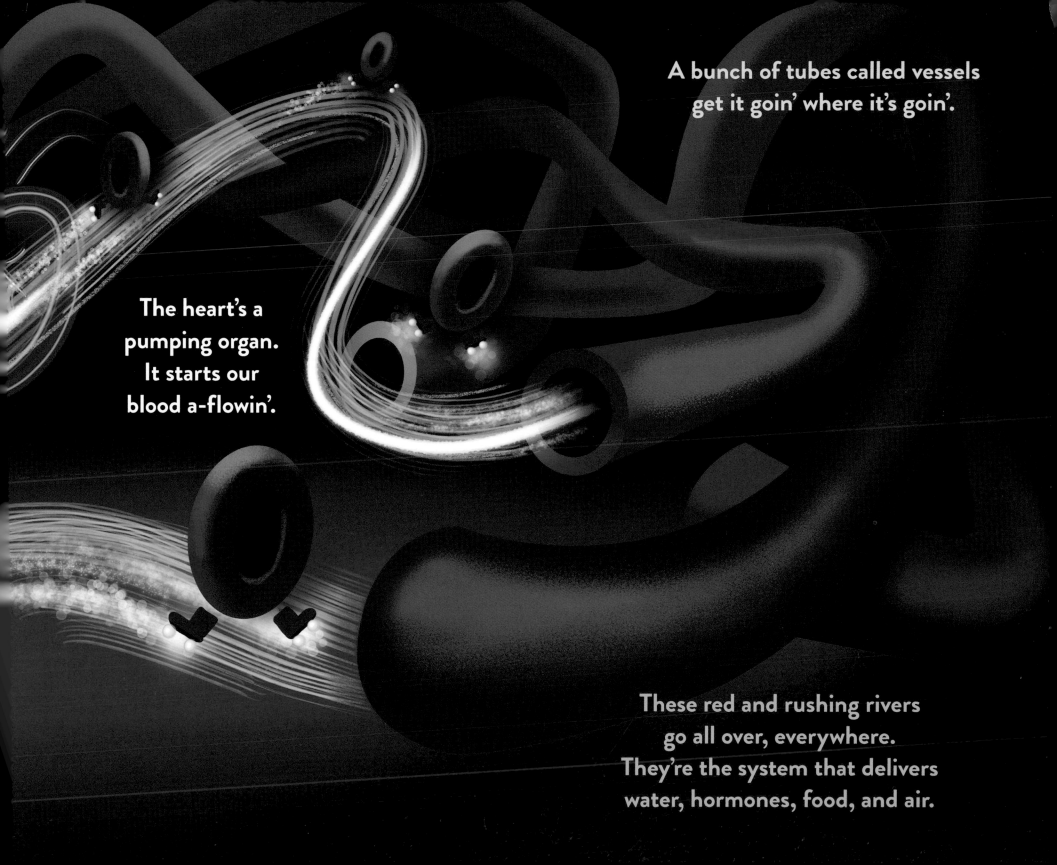

A bunch of tubes called vessels
get it goin' where it's goin'.

The heart's a
pumping organ.
It starts our
blood a-flowin'.

These red and rushing rivers
go all over, everywhere.
They're the system that delivers
water, hormones, food, and air.

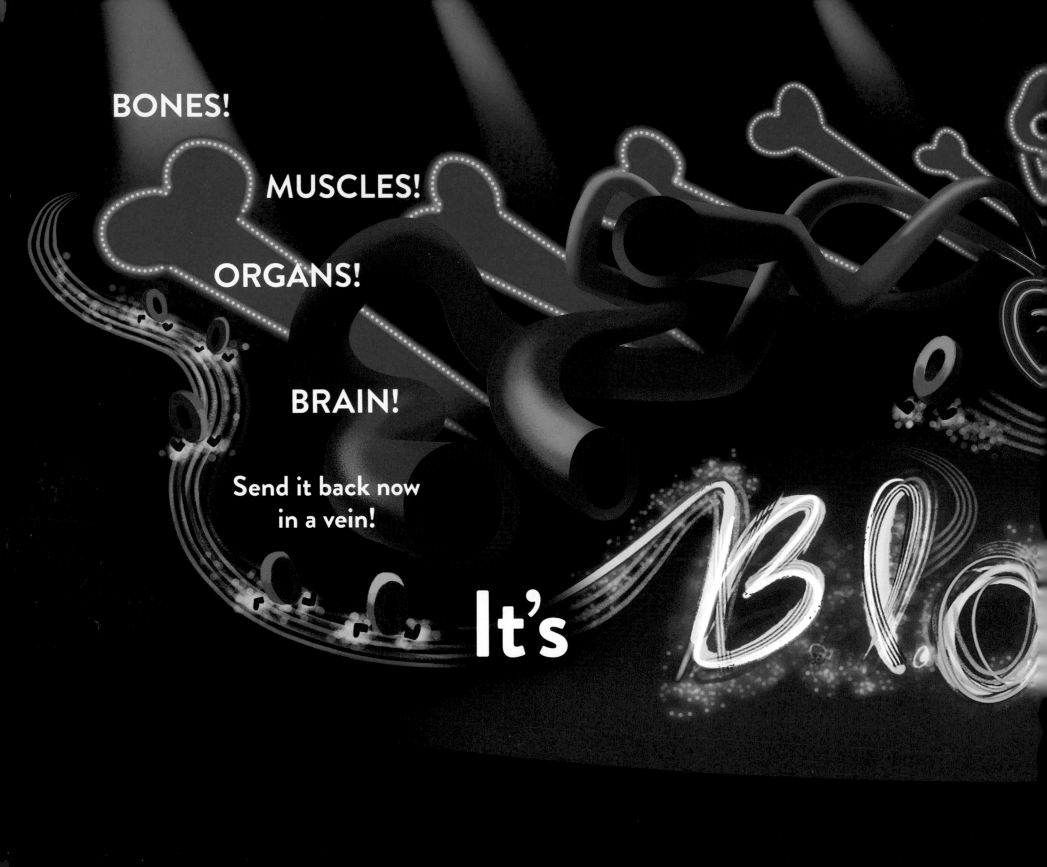

BONES!

MUSCLES!

ORGANS!

BRAIN!

Send it back now
in a vein!

It's Blo

It's blood!

(lub-dub, lub-dub)

(lub-dub, lub-dub)

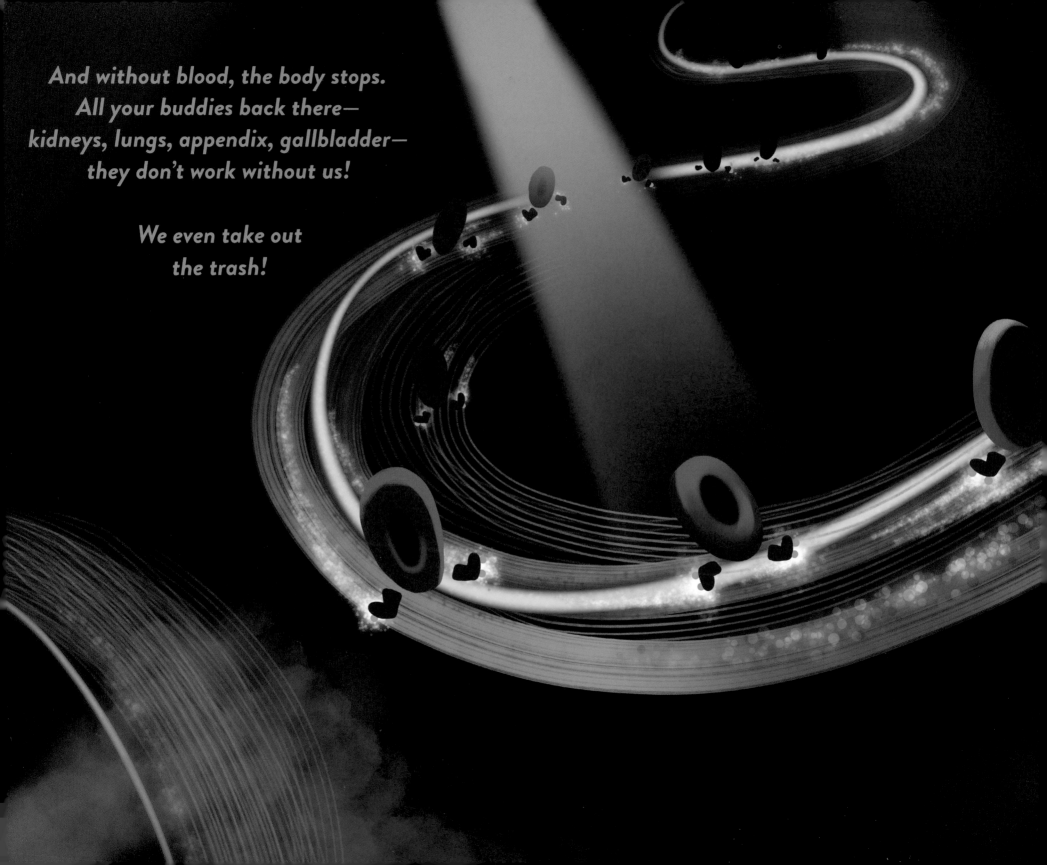

And without blood, the body stops.
All your buddies back there—
kidneys, lungs, appendix, gallbladder—
they don't work without us!

We even take out
the trash!

The food that's done digestin' gets absorbed from the intestine.

Then it takes what we don't need down to the kidneys to be peed.

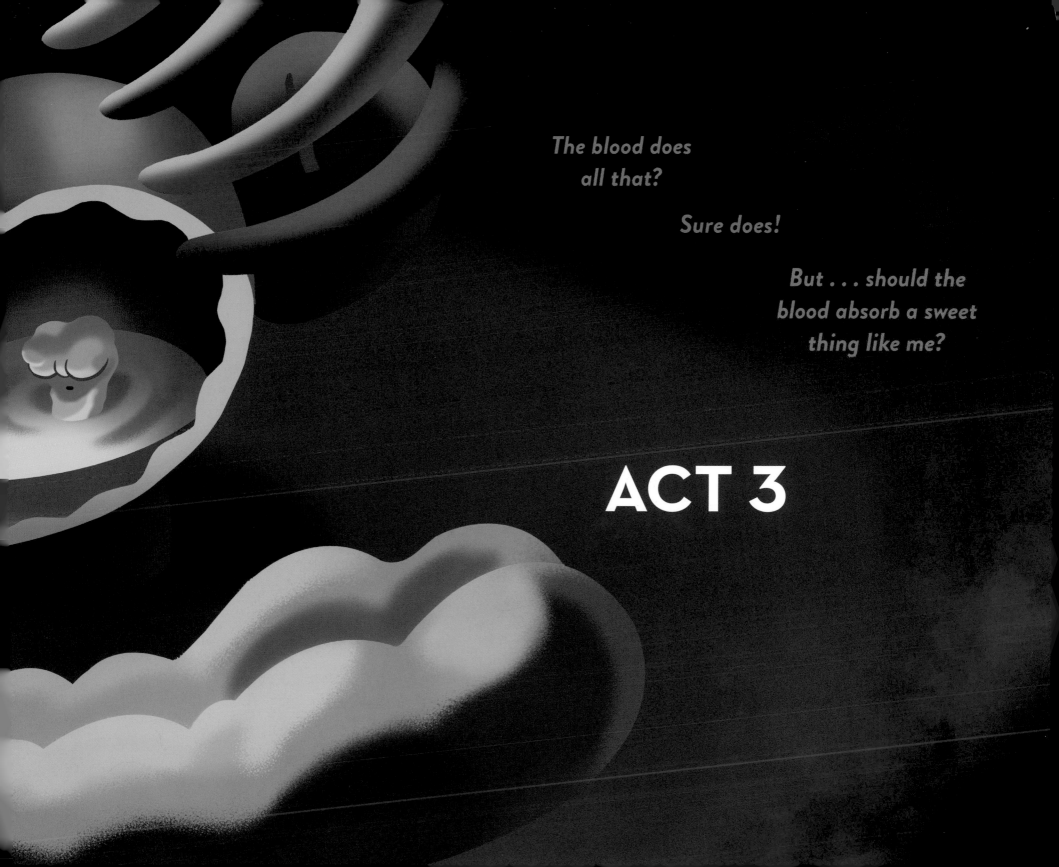

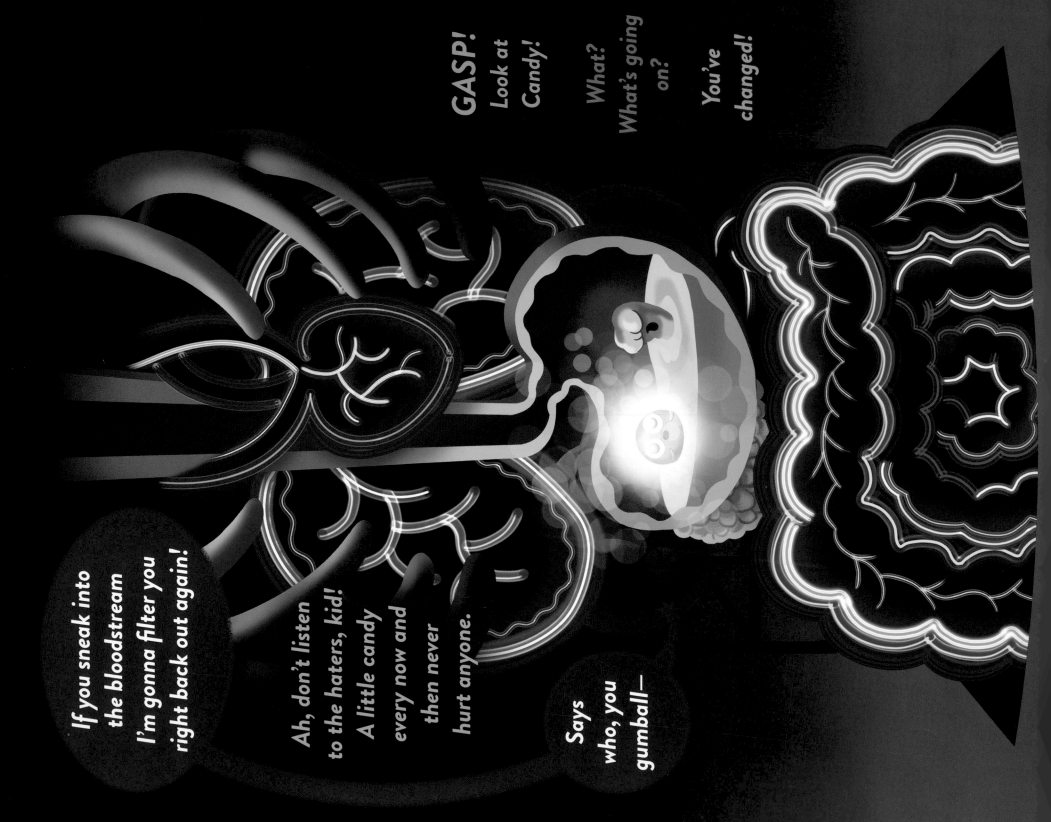

(where nobody could have seen it)

there's a wholesome, healthy peanut!

Ohmygosh! I didn't know it! I was candy, but below it

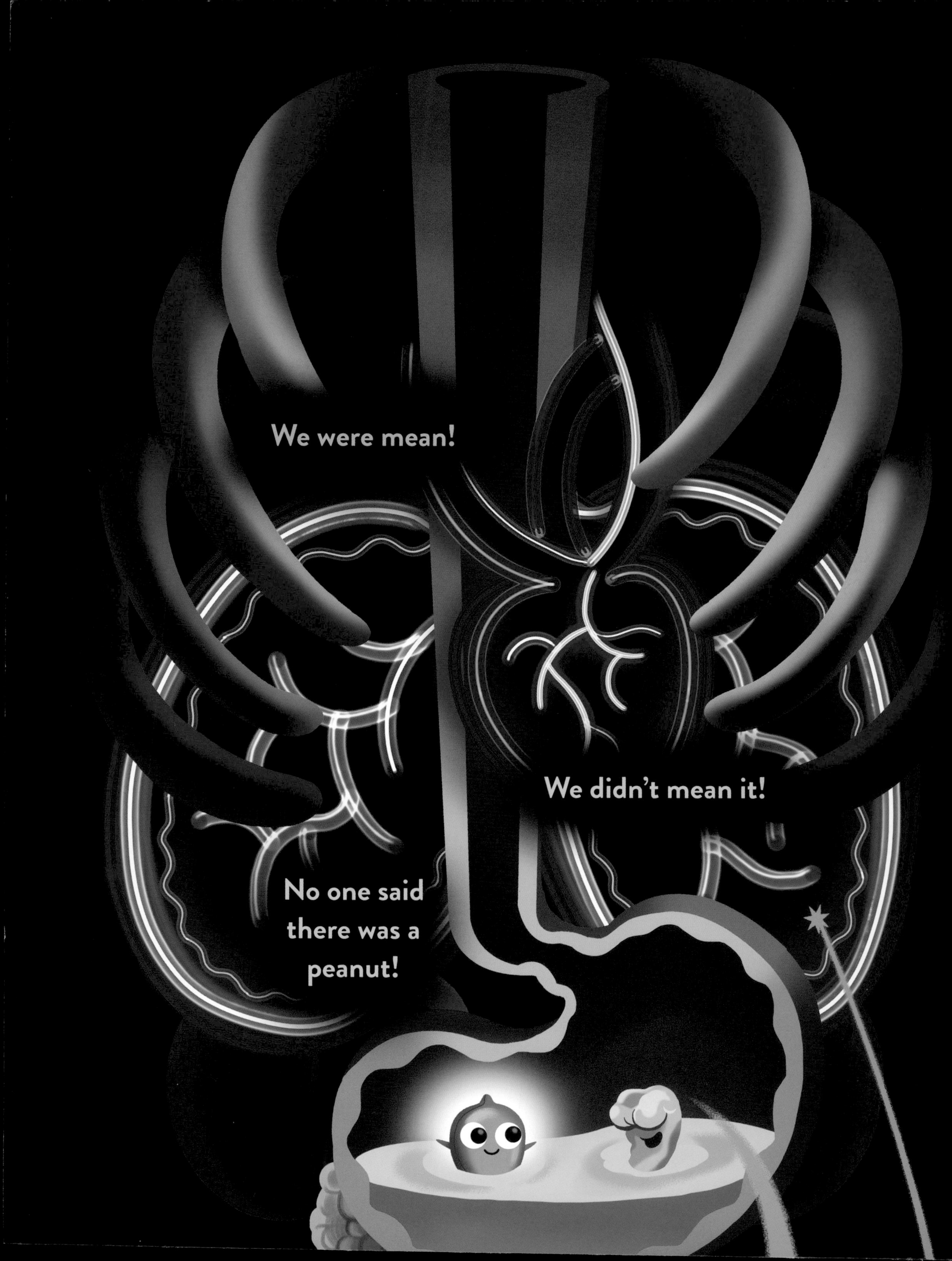
We were mean!
We didn't mean it!
No one said there was a peanut!

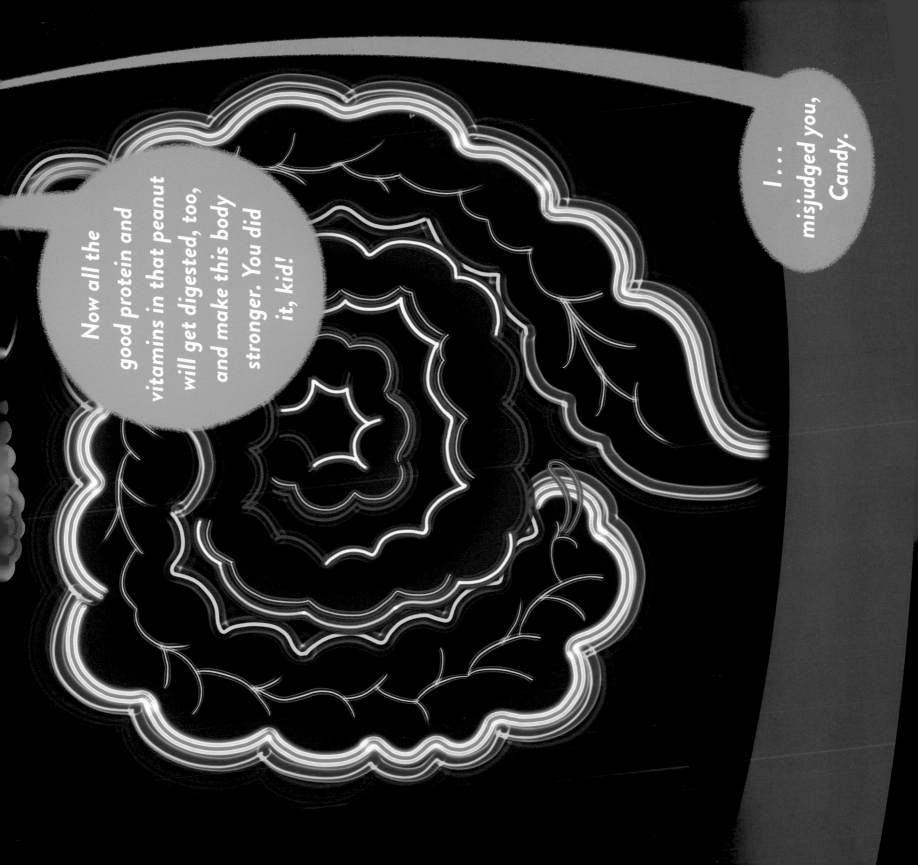

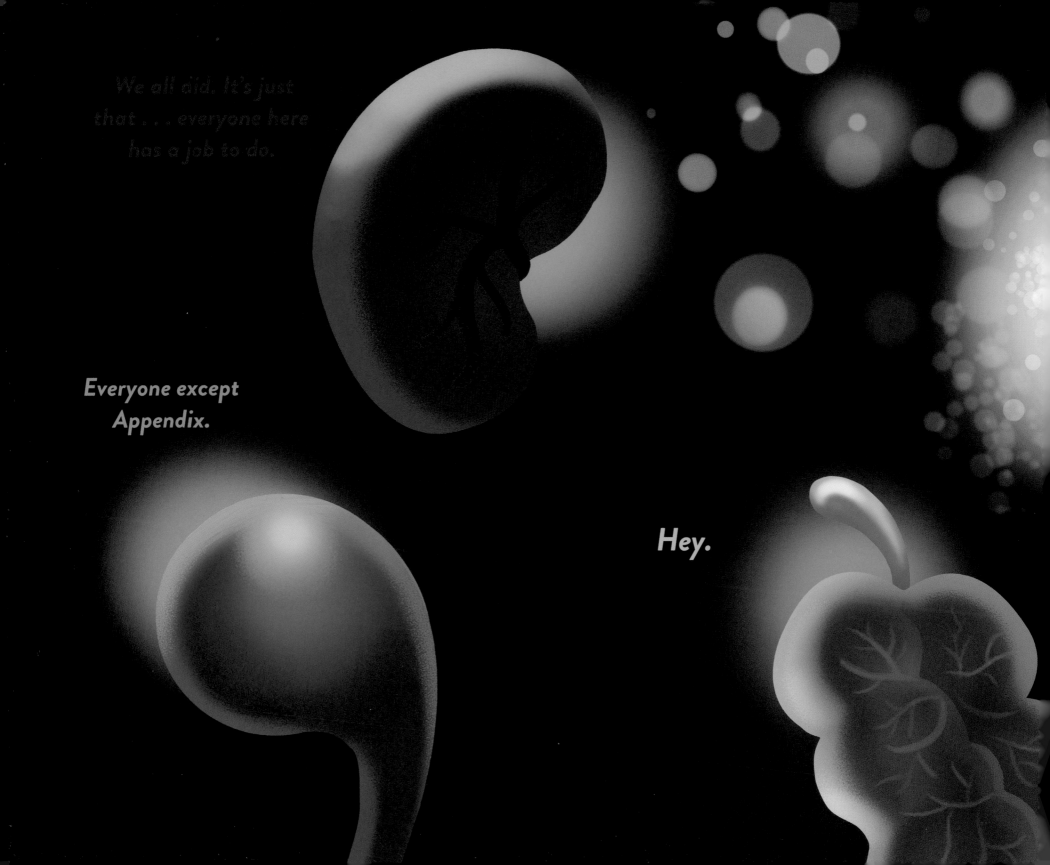

And it's hard to do
our jobs right when
people don't take care
of themselves,
you know?

Somebody has to be the
bad guy if we're going
to keep this body good
and healthy.

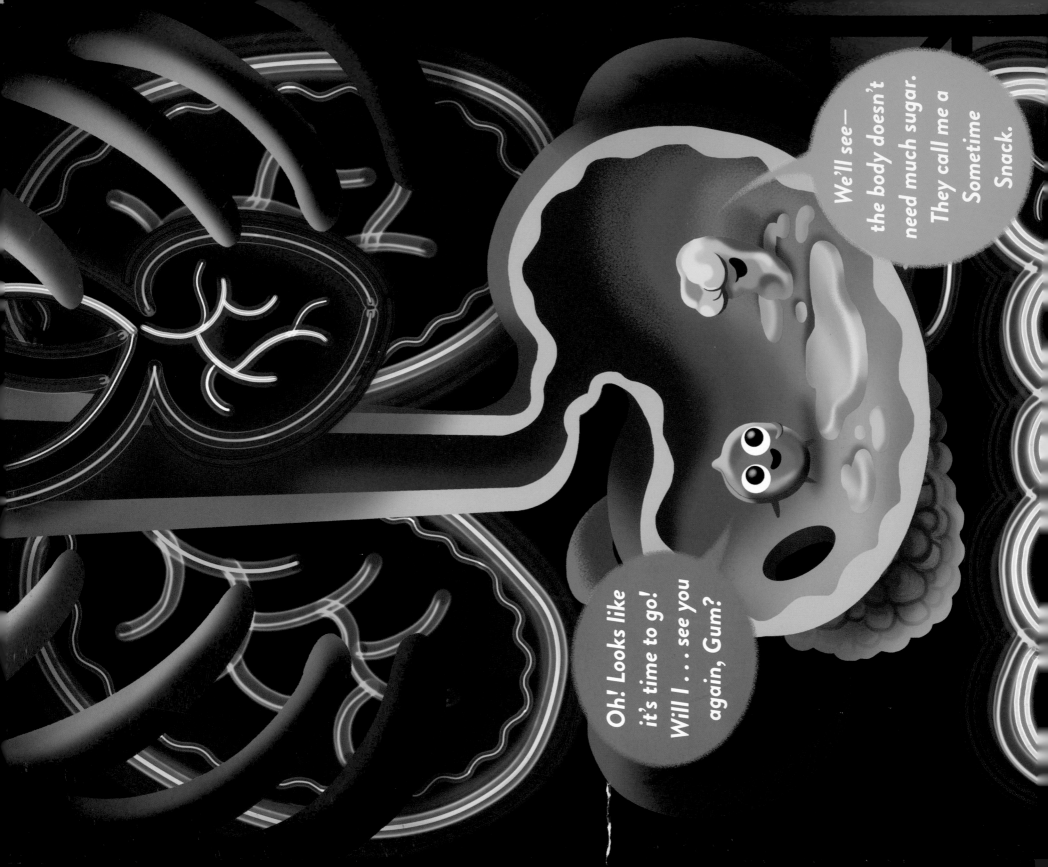

So call me sometime, Snack.

The small and large intestines
are like tunnels through your body,

and if food gets through it turns to poo
that funnels to the potty.

We've gotten to "the end," my friend,
and all that's left to do

is a big showstopping number
(and that number . . . is a two).

Well, that's our show. We've had some fun, and hopefully we've learned something.
I think you'll agree that digestion is gross and amazing.
Goodnight.

Li'l Candy's tale has ended;
now it's curtains for our show.

But let's plan to meet
next time you eat
and have another go
around the

BODY!

BODY!

BODY!

GLOSSARY

APPENDIX: A small, tube-shaped organ attached to the large intestine.

BLOOD: A red liquid that flows throughout the body, delivering oxygen and nutrients and collecting waste for removal. The blood contains

PLASMA: The fluid that blood cells float in.

PLATELETS: Cell pieces that make clots to stop bleeding.

RED BLOOD CELLS: Cells that deliver oxygen.

WHITE BLOOD CELLS: Cells that fight infection and disease.

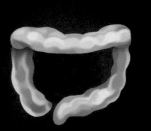

DUODENUM: The first part of the small intestine.

ESOPHAGUS: A tube that connects the mouth to the stomach.

GALLBLADDER: A small sac that holds bile until it's needed in the small intestine.

KIDNEYS: Two organs just below the rib cage that take waste out of the blood and send it to be peed out of the body.

LARGE INTESTINE: A long organ that food enters after it's gone through the small intestine. Here, water is absorbed, and the waste that's left is sent down to the rectum to be pooped out.

LIVER: A large organ next to the stomach that does a lot of things, including cleaning poisons out of the body and making bile. Bile is stored in the gallbladder and sent to the small intestine, where it helps with digestion.

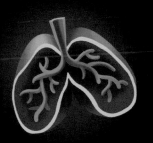

LUNGS: A pair of organs inside the chest. They take oxygen out of the air and send it to the bloodstream while pushing carbon dioxide, which we don't need, out of the body.

PALATE: The roof of the mouth.

PANCREAS: A large organ behind the stomach that makes pancreatic juice, which helps break down food. The pancreas also helps control how much sugar is in the blood.

PERISTALSIS: The flexing and relaxing of muscles in the esophagus, stomach, and intestines that moves food through the body.

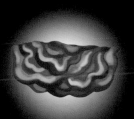

SMALL INTESTINE: A long, twisty organ where food goes after it's gone through the stomach. The small intestine is where most of the helpful nutrients are absorbed from food.

STOMACH: A hollow organ between the esophagus and the small intestine that partially digests food. The stomach mixes food with enzymes and acids that break the food down.

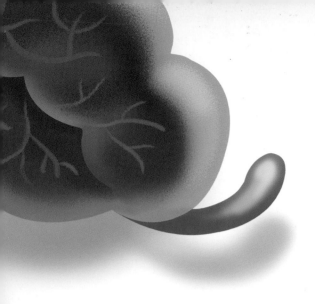

APPENDIX

Hello, yes, I just want to say that doctors no longer believe the appendix is useless—
I am now understood to be a safe place for good bacteria.

A "safe place."

Okay, thank you.

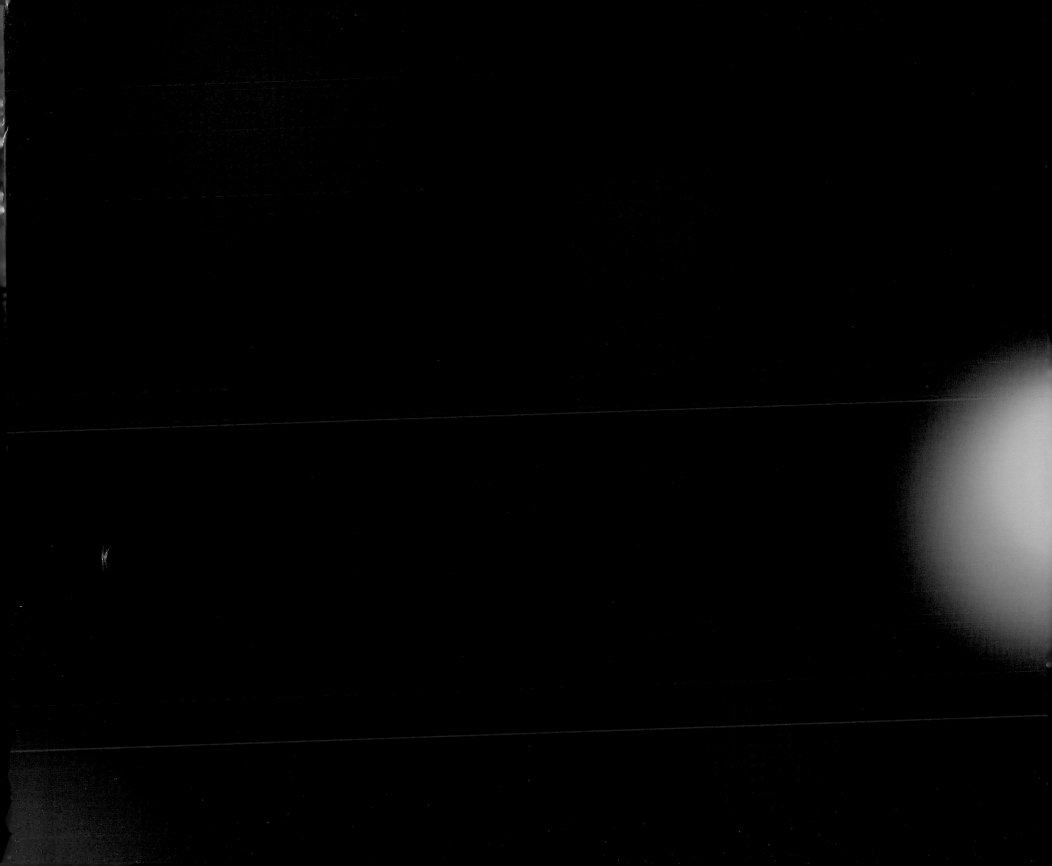